Richard Scarry's
COLORS

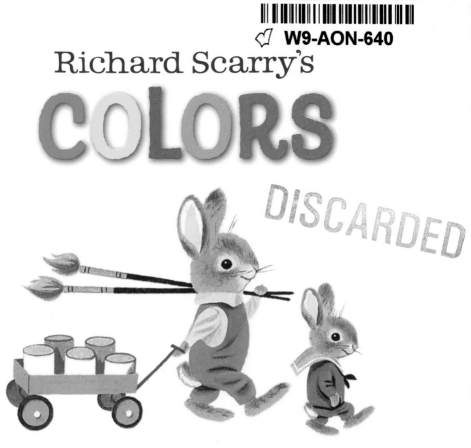

By Kathleen N. Daly

Published on the occasion of the 75th anniversary of Little Golden Books

A GOLDEN BOOK • NEW YORK

randomhousekids.com
Educators and librarians, for a variety of teaching tools, visit us at RHTeachersLibrarians.com
Library of Congress Control Number: 2015953476
ISBN 978-0-399-55367-7 (trade)
MANUFACTURED IN CHINA
10 9 8 7 6 5 4 3 2 1

This color is yellow.

Baby chicks are yellow.
Daffodils are yellow, too.

This color
is blue.

A kitten's eyes are blue.

The sky is blue, and
so are noisy blue jays.

This color is red.

An apple is red.

This tricycle is red.

Blue and yellow make green.

A fat frog is green.

In summer,
leaves are green.

Red and yellow
make orange.

Bunny's carrot
is orange.

A pumpkin is orange, too.

Blue and red make purple.

Violets and pansies are purple.

Grapes and plums
are purple.

This color is brown.

Red   Yellow   Blue   Black

make brown.

Puppy's fur is brown.

This little pony
is brown, too.

Red and white make pink.

Roses and bunny noses
are pink.

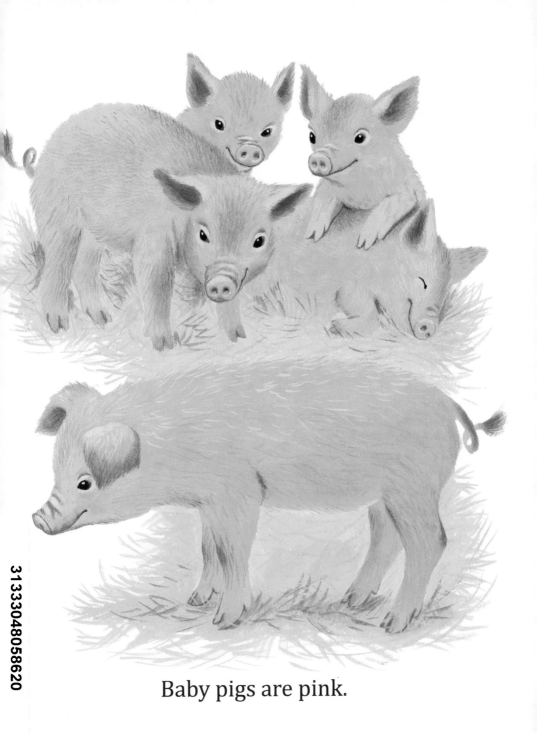

Baby pigs are pink.

This is white.

A snowman is white,
and so is a duck.

This is black.

Sleepy bear cubs
are black.

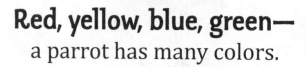

Red, yellow, blue, green—
a parrot has many colors.

Which is your favorite color?